The Sasquatch, the Fire and the Cedar Baskets

THE — SASQUATCH, THE FIRE AND THE CEDAR BASKETS

JOSEPH DANDURAND

WITH ILLUSTRATIONS BY
SIMON DANIEL JAMES

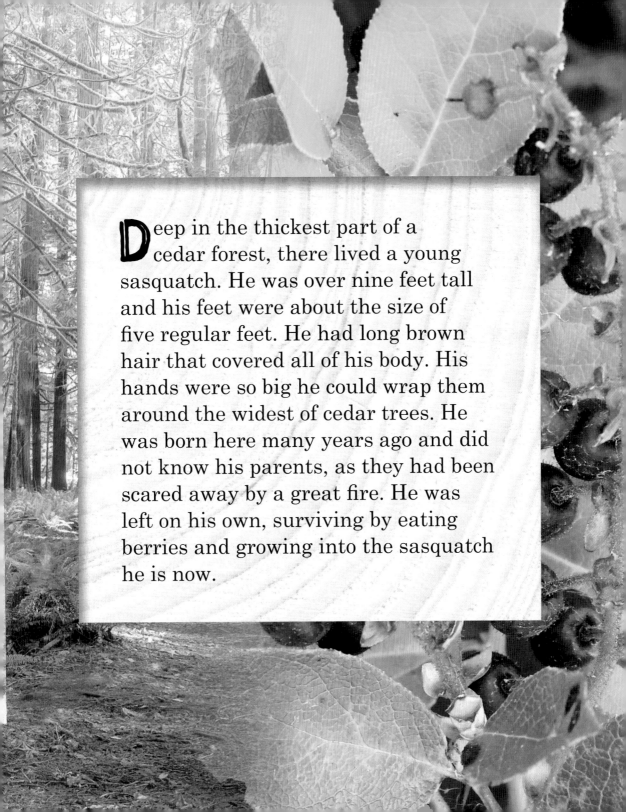

Deep in the thickest part of a cedar forest, there lived a young sasquatch. He was over nine feet tall and his feet were about the size of five regular feet. He had long brown hair that covered all of his body. His hands were so big he could wrap them around the widest of cedar trees. He was born here many years ago and did not know his parents, as they had been scared away by a great fire. He was left on his own, surviving by eating berries and growing into the sasquatch he is now.

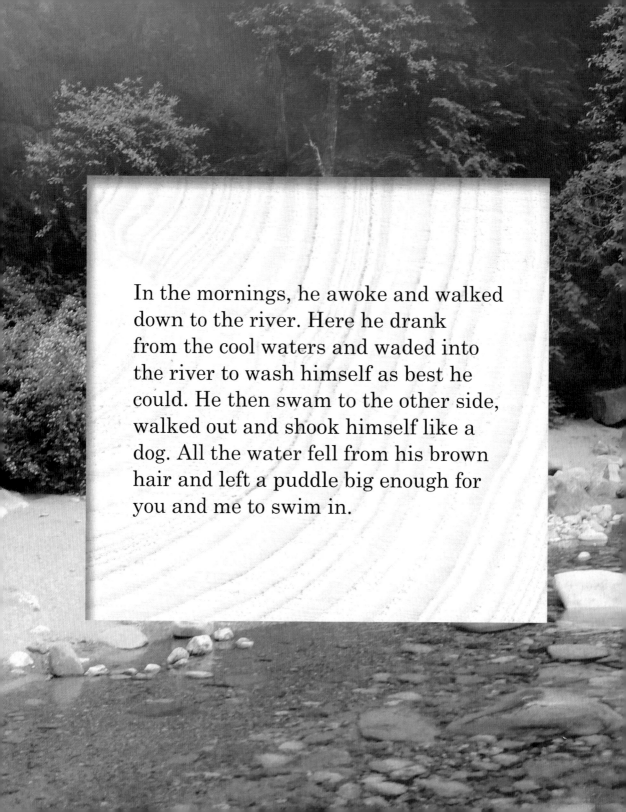

In the mornings, he awoke and walked
down to the river. Here he drank
from the cool waters and waded into
the river to wash himself as best he
could. He then swam to the other side,
walked out and shook himself like a
dog. All the water fell from his brown
hair and left a puddle big enough for
you and me to swim in.

Then he walked into the forest and
looked for mushrooms and moss to
eat. He looked for special flowers that
helped him stay healthy and warm.
He sat and stared at his big feet and
wondered why the world around him
was so interested in his feet, and why
they always chased him when
they saw him. He was too fast to
catch, but what would they do
if they ever got him?

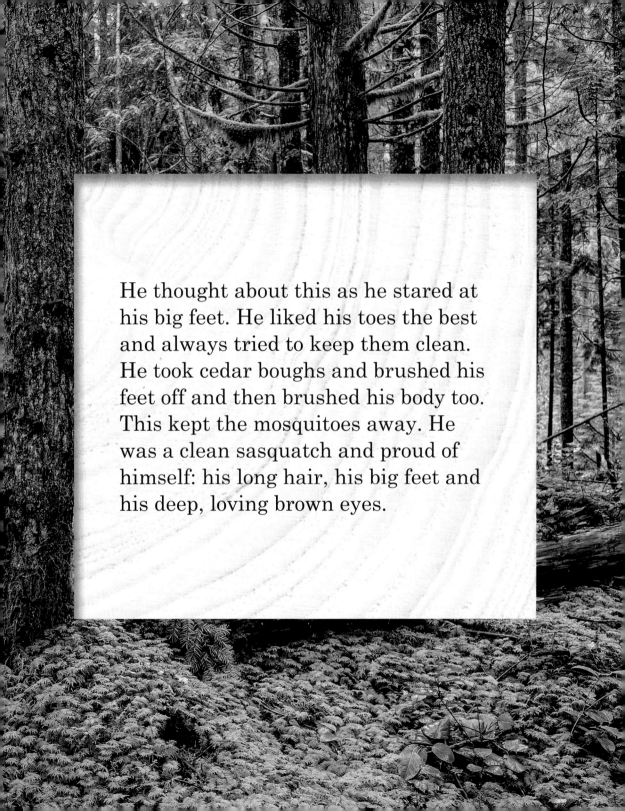

He thought about this as he stared at his big feet. He liked his toes the best and always tried to keep them clean. He took cedar boughs and brushed his feet off and then brushed his body too. This kept the mosquitoes away. He was a clean sasquatch and proud of himself: his long hair, his big feet and his deep, loving brown eyes.

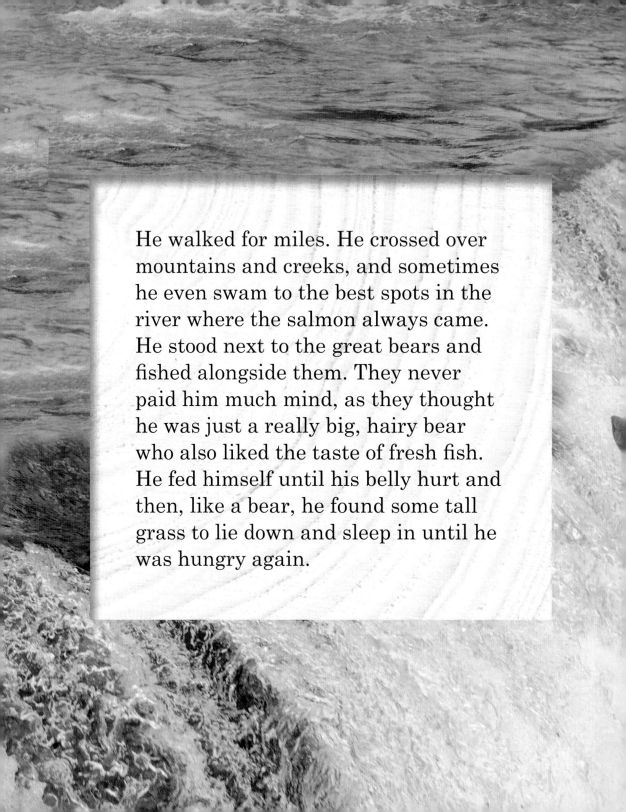

He walked for miles. He crossed over
mountains and creeks, and sometimes
he even swam to the best spots in the
river where the salmon always came.
He stood next to the great bears and
fished alongside them. They never
paid him much mind, as they thought
he was just a really big, hairy bear
who also liked the taste of fresh fish.
He fed himself until his belly hurt and
then, like a bear, he found some tall
grass to lie down and sleep in until he
was hungry again.

This went on all summer until the fish were no more, and then he swam back across the rivers and walked across the highest mountains. All along the way, he left his giant footsteps, and sometimes you could see them in the dirt and snow, but most times the rain came and washed them away.

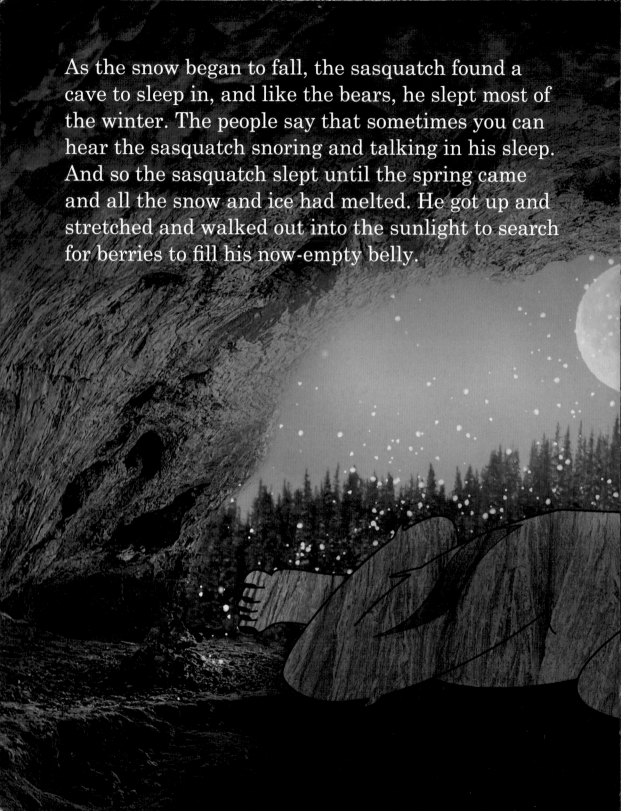

As the snow began to fall, the sasquatch found a cave to sleep in, and like the bears, he slept most of the winter. The people say that sometimes you can hear the sasquatch snoring and talking in his sleep. And so the sasquatch slept until the spring came and all the snow and ice had melted. He got up and stretched and walked out into the sunlight to search for berries to fill his now-empty belly.

Another year had passed and he was now over twelve feet tall, and his feet were now about a size twenty-five. He was slower, as he had also gained in size. His hair was longer and he was now a full-grown sasquatch. He was now a spirit of the great cedar forest. He was a beautiful sasquatch.

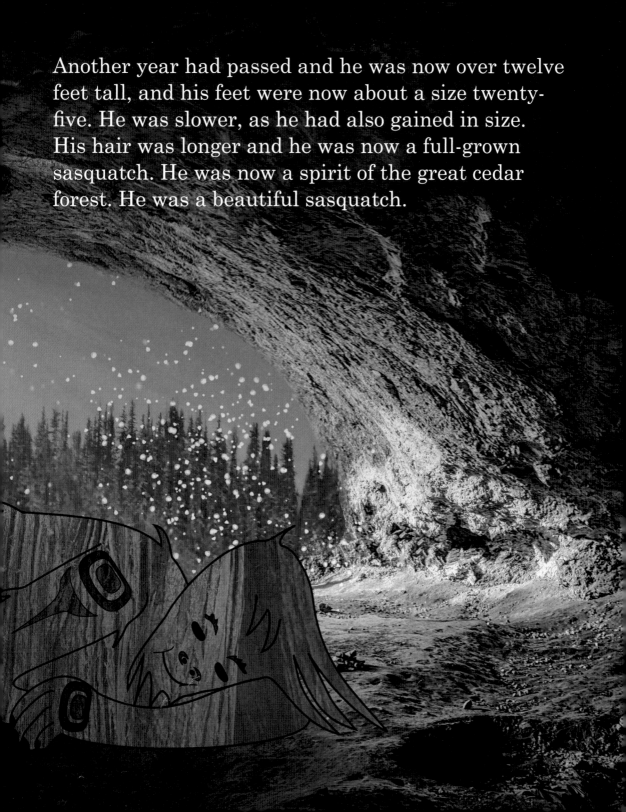

It was a hot summer's day and the sasquatch was getting a cool drink of water from a stream that was fed by the melting snow of a mountain. The sasquatch stood up because he smelled something he had never smelled before. He walked toward the smell and there, drinking from the same stream, was a lady sasquatch. She was so beautiful. She was at least nine feet tall and a lighter brown colour than he was. She turned, looked at him and smiled. She was not afraid of him as he walked toward her. She put out her hand. He took it and they both walked deeper into the stream. They stayed in the stream all day as the hot summer sun warmed the lands around them. The two sasquatches had found each other and they were happy to finally have someone to share the world with. They were, of course, in love.

It was the coldest of winters and the ground was covered with snow. The two sasquatches shared a cave, and as the months went by, the lady sasquatch made cedar baskets that were so wonderfully constructed, they could hold water and never leak. The months went by and spring came and all the snow had melted.

The two sasquatches now were three, as they had a little girl sasquatch who was already near six feet tall. She looked like her mother but with lighter brown hair. Her father loved her from the moment she was born, and together they ran up and down the mountains chasing butterflies, trying to catch them. As the two played, the mother sasquatch continued to make her cedar baskets. After each was made, it was left by a tree to gather rainwater until it was full. They were left there one by one, and soon there were thousands of cedar baskets filled with rainwater. It would be their protection. It would one day save them.

That day came during a hot summer. With the wind blowing, soon the air was full of smoke and the three sasquatches were on the move, as a great forest fire was quickly burning up the trees around them. They climbed as high as they could but the smoke was getting too thick to breathe, so they climbed higher. As far as they could see, the earth was on fire.

The sasquatch told his family to stay on the highest mountain as he went down into the heart of the fire. He could barely see and breathe, as the flames were now as hot as the sun. He began to move quickly. He went from each tree that had a cedar basket beside it and he threw each basket of water at the flames and then he would move on to the next. He threw a thousand baskets of rainwater at the flames!

Soon the fire was out and the forest smouldered in smoke. As the moon came up, the sasquatch was exhausted. He had saved his family from a great fire. He had used the beautiful baskets of cedar that the lady sasquatch had made and left by the trees. He woke up the next morning and went up the mountain to find his family. They were resting beneath the last tree of the forest.